Charlie
& The Big Snow

Look out for other books in this series:

Charlie
& The Cat Flap

Charlie
& The Great Escape

Charlie
& The Big Snow

Hilary McKay
Illustrated by Sam Hearn

SCHOLASTIC

First published in the UK in 2007
by Scholastic Children's Books
An imprint of Scholastic Ltd
Euston House, 24 Eversholt Street
London, NW1 1DB, UK
Registered office: Westfield Road, Southam, Warwickshire, CV47 0RA
SCHOLASTIC and associated logos are trademarks and or
registered trademarks of Scholastic Inc.

10 digit ISBN 0 439 96882 8
13 digit ISBN 978 0439 9688 2 9

British Library Cataloguing-in-Publication Data
A CIP catalogue record for this book is available from the British Library

Typeset by Falcon
Printed in the UK by CPI Bookmarque, Croydon, CR0 4TD
Papers used by Scholastic Children's Books are made
from wood grown in sustainable forests.

1 3 5 7 9 10 8 6 4 2

www.scholastic.co.uk/zone

Max's Fault (I)

Charlie was seven years
old when the big snow
came. It was almost the
first time in his entire life
there had ever been
enough snow to make
a snowman. The only other time
it had happened he had not been allowed out

because he was ill. He had caught the illness from his big brother, Max. Even now, a year later, he had not quite forgiven Max for this.

However, at last it had happened again. Charlie woke up and found that the bedroom he shared with Max was filled with clear cold light. White splodges patterned the window glass. The sky looked close and grey.

Snow! thought Charlie as he scrambled out of bed, and then he thought, Nobody bothered to tell me.

Charlie's father, who was always the first to be up, would already be on his way to work. His mother was in the shower; Charlie could hear the water running. Neither of them had bothered to shake Charlie awake and tell him that it had snowed at last.

That did not surprise Charlie very much, because after all they were grown-ups and did not have any sense. But it seemed to Charlie that Max should have woken him. Max was nowhere to be seen.

So even before he got to the bedroom window and looked out at the garden in the snow, Charlie was feeling a little hurt and disappointed. Looking out made him feel more disappointed than ever.

Already the clean white snow, the lovely
snow that Charlie had waited for for so
long, had been walked in.

The milkman had left a double line
of tracks across the lawn to deliver
two pints of milk to the kitchen
doorstep. Just looking at the
milkman's footprints made Charlie
mad. The milkman could easily have
walked back in his own footsteps,
leaving only a line of prints. But no,
he had made two.

That was not all. Charlie's father
went to work on the motorbike he
kept in the shed at the bottom of the
garden. He had pushed his
motorbike

all the way up the garden path, leaving a terrible trail of wheel tracks and footprints behind him. Charlie could tell that his father had not even tried to carry the motorbike instead of pushing it, so as not to damage the snow.

It was only a small garden. Already half the snow had been messed up and wasted.

Charlie rushed downstairs and into the living room. There he found his brother, Max. Max was doing his homework and recording a CD for a friend and watching TV and eating cereal all at the same time.

"Max, haven't you *seen*?" demanded Charlie, dragging open the lace curtains at the window so eagerly one of them came off in his hand. "Look!"

"Charlie!" said Max. "Mum'll go mad! Mind that plant, it's going to fall! There, I told you it would! What's the matter with you?"

"It's *snowing*!" said Charlie.

"'Course it is," said Max. "It has been for ages. Football's cancelled. Get out of the way of the TV, Charlie!"

"But you said you'd help me make a snowman!" wailed Charlie.

"Well, I will," said Max. "After school."

"Why not now?"

"There's no time now," said Max. "Not if you want to do it properly."

Charlie wanted to do it properly more

than anything, and he knew without Max's help this could not happen. Because Max was good at everything, and he, Charlie, was not. If Max decided to build a snowman, then without doubt, it would be the snowman to beat all snowmen. It was not the same with the things Charlie decided to do.

"After school we'll do it," promised Max, turning back to his homework. "Get me some orange juice, will you, Charlie?"

"Get it yourself," said Charlie crossly, and went into the kitchen to open the door and look at the snowy garden.

Suzy the cat was already outside, wandering round and round the bird table, which she had never learned she could not reach. There were black paw-prints everywhere, dozens of them, every one a wasted circle of snow.

This is terrible! thought Charlie, and he dashed up stairs and bashed on the bathroom door shouting, "Help! Help!" until his mother came out.

"Whatever is the matter, Charlie?" she exclaimed. "Are you hurt?"

"It's *snowed*!" Charlie told her.

"Oh really, Charlie!" said his mother. "Is that all? I thought something dreadful had happened!" And she went back into the bathroom and shut the door, so Charlie had to bash even harder to get her out again.

"It's all being *wasted*!" said Charlie. "Suzy's walking in it!'

"My goodness, Charlie!" grumbled his mother. "Can't I even have a shower in peace? Go and get dressed!" Then she disappeared yet again, and when Charlie hammered on the door some more she yelled at him to go away.

GO AWAY!

Charlie went back to Max, who was now eating a jam sandwich, listening to the recording he had

made and gelling up his hair with the help of his reflection in the TV screen.

"The snow's all getting wasted!" complained Charlie. "What'll we do? It will never last till after school!"

"Shove it in the freezer!" said Max, pulling the front of his hair into little spikes with a mixture of jam and gel.

Max said afterwards that he had been joking.

Charlie's Mother's Fault

Charlie went back to the kitchen and looked at the snow again. He wondered how long it would actually take to shove it in the freezer. He didn't think he could possibly manage to rescue it all. However, he admitted to himself that, like all Max's ideas, it was pretty good. Much better than doing nothing, anyway.

At first Charlie only intended to save enough to make one reasonably-sized snowman. But then he got interested in the job, and could not bear to stop. In his pyjamas and slippers he shovelled carrier bags full of snow and packed them into all the empty spaces of the freezer until the door would hardly shut. In fact, it would not shut, but Charlie did not notice that. Nobody did until much later in the day.

When the freezer would hold no more he filled up the salad box at the bottom of the fridge. He also balanced odd snowballs among the eggs and cheese and yoghurt and things. In this way Charlie got most of the snow in the garden into a safe cold place before his mother came out of the bathroom.

It was Charlie's mother's fault that he was so late for school. She caught him on the stairs and saw the state of him.

"You've been *outside*!" she squealed.

"Only a little bit," said Charlie, hoping to calm her down. "And I've been inside too. Outside and inside. . ."

"*You've been playing in the snow!*"

"Not playing!" said Charlie.

"In your pyjamas!"

"I didn't think you'd want me to get my school clothes wet," explained Charlie, angelically. "Your hair looks nice! I like your jumper! Would you like me to get you some toast and orange juice?"

"I don't believe I am standing here listening to this!" said Charlie's mother, and she seized him and dragged him to the bathroom and would not let him out until he

had had a hot bath and got
all the mud off, and turned
a pinkish colour again.
Instead of blue. Then she made
him put on an incredible amount
of clothes, and marched him down
to the kitchen where she
discovered the state of
the fridge.

Already the snowballs were
melting and dripping on
everything inside.

"WELL!" said Charlie's mother in a very
shocked voice. "And what have you to say
about this, Charlie?"

"Well!" said Charlie, equally shocked.
"What a rotten fridge! It's ruined all my
snowballs! You should complain to the
fridge makers!"

Charlie's mother did not complain to the fridge makers. She complained to Charlie instead. As she complained she furiously cleaned out the fridge saying, "Snow, snow, it comes every year! I can't stand the stuff! Max was never the trouble that you are!"

"It was Max's fault!" protested Charlie. "It was his idea! It was Max who said to shove it in. . ."

Then Charlie suddenly shut up. He thought it might be a good thing to keep the snow in the freezer private. He was glad Max was out of the way, gone to big school on the school bus. He said, to change the subject, "I don't mind if I don't go to school today. I could stay at home and do all the work."

"Ha!" said Charlie's mother, and drove him furiously to school. She took him right into his classroom, where he had already been marked absent.

"Oh hello, Charlie!" said Charlie's teacher, not looking very pleased to see them.

Charlie's mother said hello to the teacher, and she said that she was very sorry Charlie was late, and that Charlie would have to have school dinners because they had come out in such a rush they had forgotten his school bag and his packed lunch.

Just as she was leaving she added, "And if he had any homework I'm afraid he's forgotten that too!"

Charlie could hardly believe his ears. His own mother reminding his teacher about his homework! He wanted to ask her, "Whose side are you on?"

What happened next was definitely

Charlie's mother's fault.

Homework had been to find out what it would have been like to be a boy or girl growing up in Roman times. Charlie had not found anything out. He had not even thought about it.

"Well," said Charlie's teacher when his mother had gone. "Charlie. Even if your homework has been left at home you can still *tell* us about what it was like to be a boy growing up in Roman times. I hope."

Charlie hoped so too, because she looked very Monday morningish and cross. He thought very quickly, and then he told the class that life in Roman times would have been totally boring. There were no PlayStations, said Charlie, no football and no TV.

hissssssss

"Tell us what things there *were*!" said his teacher.

Charlie ignored her and said there were no cinemas or computers or car racetracks.

"Were there any sort of racetracks?" asked his teacher hopefully.

Charlie said there were no skateboards or Rollerblades or mountain bikes, and a lot of people started giggling.

Charlie loved to hear the class giggling, and he felt he was doing very well on how totally boring life was for a boy in Roman times, so he looked around the classroom and said there were no paint pots or reading corners or guinea pigs.

The class giggled more than ever. It was their fault the teacher got so annoyed. But it was Charlie she was annoyed with. She said she thought he had not bothered to do any homework at all. Just like last week, when he had not written a Viking Packing List of everything a Viking would need to take when his longship was going to invade an unknown shore. And just like the week before, when Charlie had not drawn a map of dinosaur country with the swamps and ferns and dinosaurs clearly labelled.

In fact, said Charlie's teacher, she could not remember when Charlie ever *had* done his homework.

At break time everyone went out to play in the snow. More had fallen since school started, enough for snowballs and snow slides and snowmen, too. But Charlie was not out there to enjoy it. He had missed his chance again.

Charlie had to stay in the classroom with a book about the totally boring Romans.

Not The Guinea Pig's Fault

Charlie said afterwards that what happened at break time was the Romans' fault for being so boring that he could not bear to do his homework, and the class's fault for giggling and making the teacher annoyed, and the teacher's fault for keeping him in with the totally boring Romans.

He said it was not the guinea pig's fault.

Break time began with Charlie and the teacher and her mug of coffee and a pile of books about Roman Times all together in the classroom. Outside it was snowy and wonderful. In the playground Charlie's friend Henry was making snowballs.

Henry was sorry for Charlie, and he wanted to make him smile. That was why he began throwing his snowballs accidentally-on-purpose towards the

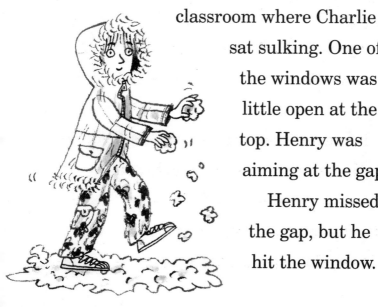

classroom where Charlie sat sulking. One of the windows was a little open at the top. Henry was aiming at the gap.

Henry missed the gap, but he hit the window.

Bump! And then again.

Bump! And then again, and by this time the teacher was on her feet. She said, "I am just going outside, Charlie. I may be some time," and hurried out of the classroom to tell Henry what she thought of him.

When she was gone Charlie gave up pretending to look at the Roman books. Instead, he began wandering around the classroom. His favourite place was the pet corner, where the stick insects lived in their big glass tank and 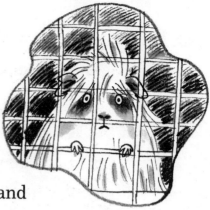 Smudge the guinea pig had his cage.

Smudge's bag of guinea pig food was kept beside his cage.

Another thing that had been forgotten that morning, as well as the school bag and packed lunch and homework, was Charlie's breakfast. So now Charlie was very hungry, and he tried a small handful of guinea pig food and found it was not bad at all. It was a mixture of little orange and red biscuits, peanuts, hard crunchy cornflakes and dark green pellets that tasted bitter and dry. Charlie chomped his way through one handful, and started on another, carefully picking out the dark green pellets first. He offered them to the guinea pig, but he did not seem to like them either.

"Yes, well," said Charlie to the guinea pig. "I'll tell you why I'm here! Because of the rotten boring Romans who I didn't do my homework about. Which no one would have noticed if Mum hadn't brought me in so late and told everyone about me not having my school bag and homework and no packed lunch either."

Charlie paused and took another handful of guinea pig food and asked the guinea pig, "Do you mind me eating this?"

The guinea pig looked like he could not care less what Charlie ate. He did not seem particularly interested in Charlie's grumbles either, but Charlie carried on anyway.

"And the reason I was late, with no packed lunch and everything was because of Mum moaning about snow in the fridge. Which I put there before it all got wasted with people walking on it. Even the cat. What's the matter with putting snow in the fridge, anyway? Snow's clean and the fridge is cold!"

The guinea pig, looking dreadfully bored, scratched an ear with a back leg in a desperate kind of way.

"I wouldn't have had to put the snow in

the fridge (which was Max's idea, only he said freezer) if anyone had told me it was snowing and got me up in time to make a snowman. But they didn't. Dad didn't. Mum didn't. Not even Max!

"Not even Max," repeated Charlie, picking out a few more guinea pig cornflakes. "I hope guinea pig food is not poisonous to humans."

The guinea pig turned and went to bed as if he did not want to discuss the subject.

Charlie waited a while, but he didn't come out again.

Then Charlie went and sat with his head in his arms until the teacher came back with the class.

She had snow in her hair and she was not in a good temper. She took no notice of Charlie until she had told Henry and several other people what she thought was the difference between a joke and just plain rudeness. Then she asked, "Is everything all right, Charlie?" as if she was not expecting to hear any good news.

"Is guinea pig food poisonous to humans?" asked Charlie. "I ate some."

"Charlie!" exclaimed the teacher. "Are you telling me that I can't leave you alone in the classroom for five minutes without you eating the guinea pig food?"

"Yes," said Charlie.

"How *much* did you eat?" demanded the teacher.

"An awful lot," said Charlie.

"Well, I don't suppose it will hurt you," said his teacher. "What did you manage to find out about the Romans while I was away?"

"I've got tummy ache,"
said Charlie.

"Charlie!"

"And I think I
feel sick," said Charlie.

The Man With the Tool Bag's Fault

If there was one thing Charlie's teacher could not bear it was children being sick in class. So Charlie had to go and lie down on the plastic sofa in the little room that opened out of the secretary's office. They gave him a blanket and a bucket and the secretary said, "I'll leave the door open. Call me if you need to but I expect I'll know."

31

Charlie lay down on the sofa and he listened to the humming sound that came from the warm classrooms full of children working, and he watched the snow falling outside the window. After a while a man came in with a tool bag, and when he saw Charlie he said, "Hello, mate!"

"Hello," said Charlie.

"You in trouble, mate?" asked the man.

"I've got to lie here with this bucket in case I'm sick," said Charlie.

The man stepped away a little and looked back through the door at the secretary.

"It's nothing catching!" she called. "He ate the guinea pig food!"

"You never did!" said the man to Charlie.

"Yes I did," said Charlie, and while the man opened his tool bag and began working on the red box that contained the fire alarm which he had come to mend, he proceeded to tell him the story of how he came to end up on the sofa with the blanket and the bucket. And by the time Charlie had finished, the fire alarm was fixed and the man began repacking his tools again.

"I've never heard anything like it!" he said to Charlie, when he had heard the whole story. "But if you ask me, you should never have eaten that guinea pig food! You should have waited."

"Till what?"

"Dinner," said the man, getting up and rubbing his knees. "Now then, I'm finished here! Don't you go pushing that little red button I've just fixed or you'll have all your class and 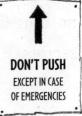 the teachers and the secretary and I don't know who else out in the snow turning a lovely shade of blue. And I hope you're feeling better soon, mate!"

Then he left.

Afterwards, when Charlie repeated what the man had said, he missed out one word. Which was Don't. Charlie said he had not heard the man say Don't. But he had heard all the rest. And lying on the sofa, getting more and more bored, he decided that what

the man had wanted was for him, Charlie,
to test the fire alarm and see if it was
working.

When Charlie had worked this out he did
nothing for a while until he heard the
secretary get up to take a message to one of
the classrooms. Then he got up, crossed the
room, opened the fire alarm box with the
tiny catch at the side, pressed the red
button, shut the box,
and lay quickly
down on the
sofa with his
eyes shut and
the blanket
over his head.

Everything
went exactly as the
man had said it

would. The whole school, including Charlie, had to leave the warm classrooms, and hurry out into the snow. There they had to stand in lines while teachers called registers and counted heads and said things like: No of course the school is not on fire! Someone has been very foolish, that is all!

And: Charlie, if I see you picking up snow again you will have no playtime for a week!

And: The sooner we get this done the sooner we can go back inside!

And: One more silly question and I shall go mad!

The Big Boys' Fault

It was no time at all before Charlie was blamed for setting off the fire alarm. The secretary and Charlie's teacher found out right away. They were very cross about it. They did not believe for one moment that the man who had fixed the fire alarm had wanted Charlie to test that it was working. The bell for lunch rang, and Charlie was still being told off, and when he interrupted and asked, "What about dinner?" they both said, "I thought you felt sick!"

Charlie explained that the fresh air had made him better. Neither of them seemed particularly pleased about this good news, and they sent Charlie into dinner last in the whole school.

Being last into dinner was a very bad thing. By the time Charlie got to the

serving hatch all the chicken shapes, baked beans, chips, iced buns, pink custard and milkshakes had disappeared and there was nothing left but horrible healthy baked potatoes, salad and yoghurt.

All Charlie's friends had finished eating and gone out long ago. Charlie had to sit down with his tray at a table full of big boys he did not know.

The big boys did not usually bother with anyone from Charlie's class, but today, because of the fire alarm, they were very friendly to Charlie. They paused their gobbling of iced buns and pink custard to say, "Nice one, Charlie!" and other cheering things like that. They said it was bad luck for poor Charlie having only salad and yoghurt to eat, and they offered him dips in their pink custard. They had nearly finished their lunches, but before they left they kindly showed Charlie how to ding his knife on the edge of the table and flick slices of cucumber high into the air when the dinner ladies were not looking. Then they said, "See you later, Charlie!" and went away, leaving Charlie all alone.

He had run out of cucumber by this time, so he flicked his baked potato instead. It landed with a horrible splatter, and before he knew it Charlie was back in the office again, this time with the Head of the whole school. She asked, "Can you possibly explain what is happening to you today, Charlie?"

Charlie explained that he had flicked the baked potato because he had no more of the cucumber that the big boys had taught him how to ding into the air. And he explained that he would never have had cucumber and baked potatoes to ding into the air if he had not been last of the whole school into dinner.

And the reason he was last of the whole school into dinner was because he had been kept behind to talk about the fire alarm.

Which he had set off to help the man with the tool bag.

Who he had met when resting on the plastic sofa with the bucket and blanket in the room by the secretary's office because he felt sick.

From eating guinea pig food instead of working on his totally boring Roman homework.

Which his class teacher would never have noticed he had not done if his mother had not brought him late to school and told how it had been left behind, along with his school bag and his packed lunch, because the morning had been such an awful rush.

Because of Charlie having to have an unexpected hot bath and then wait while all the snow he had put into the fridge was unpacked and thrown away.

He had put the snow in the fridge, he explained, to keep it safe until after school when Max was going to help him make a snowman.

Because there was no time in the morning to do it properly, because no one had woken him up, not his father or mother or even Max.

The Head Teacher said to Charlie that she had never heard such a load of rubbish in her life.

Charlie did not get into any more trouble at school that day. He could not. He spent the afternoon in the Head's office, right under her nose, doing nothing. He felt ill and weak with boredom.

But just before afternoon break she left him for a moment, and Charlie jumped up and hunted desperately on her desk for something to meddle with. The only thing he could find was her hole-punch, and he had just accidentally pulled the cover off the bottom and spilt about ten million tiny multicoloured circles of paper all over her carpet when she came back in.

The Head made him pick every single one of them up, and while he was doing it she telephoned Charlie's mother with a list of his crimes for the day. She did not miss any of them out. Charlie could hear the squawks of his mother on the other end of the phone at each new crime.

Then he heard the Head say to his mother, "I think it would be better for everyone if you came and took Charlie home."

Everyone's Fault Except Charlie's

Charlie was sent home from school. Max had never been sent home from school. Charlie's mother had never been sent home from school. Neither, she told Charlie, had Charlie's father. Nor had any of Charlie's ancestors, none of them. Charlie's mother was sure about that.

But Charlie was sent home from school.

The Head told Charlie's mother that she wondered if Charlie might be ill, and that she was just sending him home because she thought he might be happier there. Charlie's mother was not fooled by these kind words. Just before the Head telephoned, she had come home from work to find the freezer door had been open all morning. During that time Charlie's bulging bags of snow had turned into several dripping icicles and a small lake that had spread halfway across the kitchen floor.

Charlie's mother said, as she bundled Charlie out of office, "You don't look ill to me! Just plain naughty!" All the way along the corridor she told him about his ancestors and relations and especially Max never being sent home from school. In the cloakroom she told him about the icicles in the freezer and the lake on the kitchen floor.

"I hope my snow's all right," said Charlie, seriously worried for the first time that day. "Is it?"

"NO!" said his mother, very, very crossly.

Then they reached the door that led outside, and all in one moment Charlie forgot about the snow in the freezer. He stared and stared. He could hardly believe his good luck. A wonderful amount had fallen since lunch time. He guessed that the garden must be covered again, deeper than ever. And he was out of school early. There would be hours and hours to play in it. He said, "I'm going to make the best snowman *ever*!"

"Charlie," said his mother in a calm, quiet, terrible voice, "If you are not well enough to be at school you are not well enough to play in the snow."

"But I am well!" cried Charlie. "You said yourself I didn't look ill! They didn't send me home because I was ill! They sent me because I was bad!"

"Well," said Charlie's mother, even more calmly and quietly and terribly, "if you are too badly behaved to be at school you are certainly too badly behaved to play in the snow! Bed."

"What?"

"Bed," said Charlie's mother.

Charlie argued, but it made no difference. He tried to explain how it was not his fault he had been so bad. He began his long story about the big boys and the tool-bag man and all the other people who had managed to get him into trouble that day, but she would not listen. Then he tried roaring and crying and kicking things, and that did not work either. He was up in his bedroom, staring sulkily out of the window, when Max got home from school.

Max said, "What are you doing up here? I thought you'd be out in the snow!"

Charlie hadn't known how mad he was with Max until Max said that. Good Max, who had never been sent home from school.

Clever Max, who always did everything
well. Horrible Max, who had given him an
illness on the only day he had ever had
enough snow for a snowman. Rotten, awful
Max who had left him to sleep when it was
snowy outside. Max, the worst brother in
the world.

Charlie shouted at Max, "You are the
worst brother in the world! And it's all your
fault that I'm stuck up here!"

"Why?" asked Max.

"Because," said Charlie, blubbering hot
tears and pushing Max and snuffling and
hiccuping, "you didn't wake me up in time
to make a snowman. And then you said put
the snow in the freezer and you'd help me
later. And I did and Mum was mad and I
was late for school and she told my teacher
I'd forgotten my homework and they kept

me in at break
time and I
had to eat
the guinea
pig food
because I
never had any
breakfast and it
made me feel sick
so I had to go and lie down and then a man
showed me how to test the fire alarm and I
tested it and everyone had to go outside and
they found out it was me and told me off for
so long that I had to have horrible salad
and baked potatoes with the big boys and
they showed me how to ding my cucumber
and I dinged my baked potato and it
splattered all over and they sent me to the
Head's office and she rang up Mum and

said to take me home! And the snow in the freezer melted and flooded the kitchen! And whose fault is all that? Yours!" shouted Charlie.

"Yep," said Max.

Charlie stood stock still and silent, as if he had suddenly been frozen into a snowman himself. He could hardly believe his ears.

"I'm sorry," said Max.

That made Charlie start crying again, and he said, through his tears, "You said you'd help me make a snowman properly."

"I will," said Max.

Max's Fault (II)

Max always did the things he said he would do, and now he helped Charlie to make a snowman while stuck in his bedroom for outrageous behaviour. He could have begged their mother to let Charlie out. She might have said Yes, but then again she might have said No. Max did not like to make plans that depended on other people saying Yes or No.

He might have smuggled Charlie down into the garden and made a snowman there, somewhere out of sight, but that would have been sneaky. Max never did things the sneaky way. He did them properly.

Max went downstairs and checked on their mother. She was in the living room, mending the curtain. She said, "Don't go into the kitchen until the floor dries, please, Max."

"I won't," said Max.

Then he went back upstairs and opened Charlie's bedroom window wide open and he got their mother's mop bucket and he tied a long rope to it, made out of everyone's dressing-gown cords.

"Now, Charlie!" said Max, as he lowered the bucket out of the bedroom window, "all you have to do is pull!" And then he was gone.

Down in the garden Max filled the bucket with snow, and Charlie pulled it up.

And emptied it on the bedroom mat.

Over and over again.

And when they had an enormous heap of snow up in Charlie's bedroom, Max came back upstairs again and they made it into a snowman. A real, perfect snowman, with a hat and scarf and the kitchen mop for a broom.

It was so good that when it was finished Charlie could not bear not to show it to anyone. So he fetched his mother and she said, "Good heavens! Good grief! What have you done? Look at the floor! Snow all over! Look at that mat! Soaked! What a day! Max! I know who to blame for this! Charlie never would have dreamed of such a thing! Never!"

While she was shouting, Max got his camera and took a photograph of Charlie standing on the bedroom mat with his arm round his snowman.

Charlie's smile was even bigger

than the snowman's.

"What an awful day!" moaned Max and Charlie's mother.

Charlie was thinking, What a lovely day! I ate all that guinea pig food without being sick! I set off the fire alarm and got them all out in the snow! And then I got out of school early and Max and me made the best snowman in the world!

He looked at Max, who was now pointing the camera at their indignant mother, and he thought that Max was not such a bad brother after all.

What a brilliant day! thought Charlie.